THE EXTRAORDINARY FILES

Rocket into Space

Paul Blum

RISING★STARS

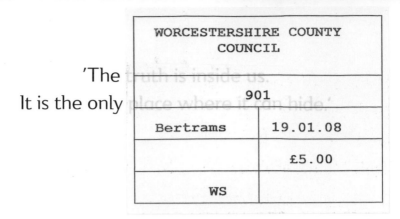

'The truth is inside us.
It is the only place where it can hide.'

WORCESTERSHIRE COUNTY COUNCIL		
	901	
Bertrams	19.01.08	
	£5.00	
WS		

nasen
Helping Everyone Achieve

nasen

NASEN House, 4/5 Amber Business Village, Amber Close,
Amington, Tamworth, Staffordshire B77 4RP

Rising Stars UK Ltd.
22 Grafton Street, London W1S 4EX
www.risingstars-uk.com

Text © Rising Stars UK Ltd.
The right of Paul Blum to be identified as the author of this work has
been asserted by him in accordance with the Copyright, Design and
Patents Act 1988.

Published 2007

Cover design: Button plc
Illustrator: Enzo Troiano
Text design and typesetting: pentacorbig
Publisher: Gill Budgell
Editor: Maoliosa Kelly
Editorial consultants: Lorraine Petersen and Cliff Moon

British Library Cataloguing in Publication Data.
A CIP record for this book is available from the British Library.

ISBN: 978 1 84680 255 3

Printed by Craft Print International Limited, Singapore

CHAPTER ONE

MI5 Headquarters, Vauxhall, London

One Sunday evening, the phones at MI5 started to ring. Hundreds of people were coming into hospitals all over north London. They had burn marks on their faces and hands.

They all told the same story. They had been walking on Hampstead Heath, near the Long Pond. At three o'clock they looked up at the sky and saw a flash of light. Two hours later, they had burn marks on their faces and hands.

The Mayor of London called a state of emergency in the city.

Time: 11,00am

Telefun

6

MCS news

Robert Parker and Laura Turnbull were secret agents who worked for MI5. They were at a big meeting in Police Headquarters. The Chief of Police was telling everyone what was happening.

"We think there may have been a terrorist attack on London. A chemical weapon or a 'dirty bomb' may have been let off over Hampstead Heath," she said.

There was a stunned silence. The police had been waiting for a terrorist attack for months. Now that it seemed to have happened, they could not believe it was true.

"You will work in teams," said the Chief of Police. "You will go into the area to calm people down. The army is guarding Hampstead Heath. You have all been trained for this day. You know what to do. Good luck."

"What shall *we* do next?" asked Agent Turnbull. "It's easy for the police. They just do as they are told."

"We're supposed to do as we are told, too," replied Agent Parker. "It's just that we don't, sometimes."

"Do you think we should report back to base, as Commander Watson told us to?" asked Turnbull.

Parker shook his head. "They won't want us to work on this case. This is a really big one. Let's go and check out Hampstead Heath for ourselves."

CHAPTER TWO

Hampstead Heath

Parker and Turnbull went to the Long Pond on Hampstead Heath.

"People swim in the Long Pond all year round," said Turnbull.

"Look at that sharp piece of metal sticking out of the water," said Parker. "Swimmers could cut themselves on that!"

Parker got the piece of metal and put it into his pocket.

"Let's get this back to the lab," he said.

Parker and Turnbull went to see Freddie, who worked in the forensic laboratory in MI5. They knew they could trust Freddie as he had helped them in the past. They needed to keep the meeting short and secret.

"Turnbull, you watch the door," Parker said.

"I'm supposed to be your boss," she said. "Why don't *you* watch the door?"

"Because you'll do it so much better than me," he said, entering the laboratory.

Parker showed Freddie the piece of metal he had taken from the pond.

"You must wear special gloves when touching that," said Freddie.

"Why?" asked Parker.

"Because it's radioactive. Anyone coming into contact with it will get radiation burns on their skin. That's what might have happened to the people in London," said Freddie.

"But what is it?" asked Parker.

"It's grade A plutonium. The only place you find it is on the night train," said Freddie.

"The night train?" asked Parker.

"The train that runs through London every night.
It takes waste from all the nuclear power stations
in England to a secret plant in north London,"
Freddie said. "I thought you were detectives.
How come you didn't know that?"

17

"Don't forget we work for the Secret Service. We're the last people to know any real secrets," Parker joked.

"But London is a city with ten million people," Turnbull said. "How can they risk running a train through it with nuclear waste on board? What if there was an accident?"

"Maybe there just has been," said Parker. "We need to check out this night train right away."

CHAPTER THREE

The agents waited until it was dark, then climbed on to the railway track.

"We're probably wasting our time, Parker," said Turnbull. "You heard it on the news. The explosion was caused by a terrorist bomb. It was left in a bin on Hampstead Heath."

"Wise up, Turnbull!" said Parker. "When will you learn that what they say is never the truth! That bit of metal must have come from the night train. There was no bomb."

Just then, the two agents heard the sound of the train coming. Parker waved goodbye to Turnbull and jumped on to the train as it slowed down.

"I'll be back for breakfast," he said. "Go and see Commander Watson now. Tell him that we've been helping the police to search Hampstead Heath."

Parker stayed on the train for an hour. The train went into a long tunnel and stopped outside what looked like a factory.

Suddenly, searchlights came on. Parker looked down and saw a huge pool. There were long pieces of metal in the water. They looked like the piece of metal he had found in the Long Pond.

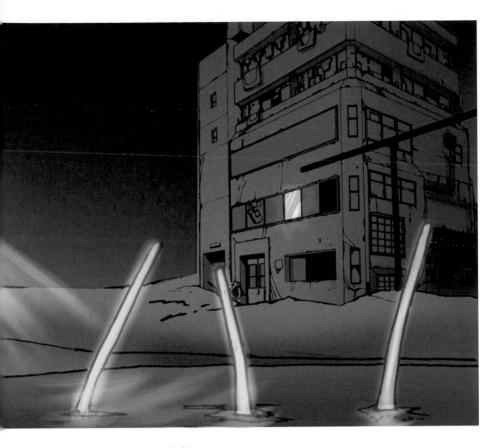

"Plutonium rods!" he whispered.

At the end of the pool there was a tall building. There was a light on in one of the windows. Parker knew he had to be quick. He was sure he was in great danger but he had to see what was in the pool.

CHAPTER FOUR

Laura Turnbull went back to her flat. She was glad
to be at home. As she put her feet up on the sofa,
she saw the shape of a man in the shadows.
She jumped out of her chair into a karate position.

"Don't do anything silly, Agent Turnbull," said
a man's voice.

Turnbull tried to see his face but there was just
darkness where his eyes should have been.
She looked down at the man's hands. He was
polishing his glasses slowly and carefully.

"How do you know my name? What do you want?
Who are you?" she shouted.

"Let's just say that my name is X," he replied.

"Look X, if you don't walk out of my flat now,
you'll have to crawl out. I'm a black belt
karate champion," she said.

"I know you are. In fact I know a lot of things about you and Agent Parker," he said. "Let me tell you some of them."

Turnbull was silent.

"You're following up a lead about the bomb on Hampstead Heath. Agent Parker has gone for a ride on the night train," he said.

"How do you know that?" cried Agent Turnbull. She tried to take a look at his face.

"Get back!" he commanded.

There was something in his voice that made Turnbull afraid. She looked down at his hands. He was polishing his glasses again.

"The Secret Service wants you to obey orders. You must leave this case alone. The bomb that went off today was planted by terrorists and it's our job to catch them. Parker isn't helping us to do that. He's sticking his nose in where it's not wanted."

"But he's only trying to find out the truth," said Turnbull.

X laughed. He was polishing his glasses so hard that Agent Turnbull thought they would break.

"Let *us* judge what is the truth," he said. "We have all the facts and you don't. If Parker keeps on sticking his nose into this case, something bad might happen to him."

"Do *you* work for the Secret Service?" she asked.

He laughed then he put on his glasses and leaned forward in his chair. Behind his glasses, there were no eyes, just empty eye sockets.

"The Secret Service works for *me*," he replied coldly.

Turnbull was frozen with horror as X stood up and walked out of her flat.

Parker came back at breakfast time.
Turnbull was glad to see him.
She told him all about X.

"I think he wants to kill us. We must
tell Commander Watson at once,"
said Turnbull.

Parker shook his head. "Commander
Watson cannot be trusted. We don't
want any of them to see that we're
frightened. We'll have to go to
somebody in the Secret Service we
can trust."

Turnbull nodded. "I'm sure Freddie
would help us," she said.

"We need to go back to Hampstead
Heath," said Parker. "I saw something
last night that looked like a rocket or
a missile. Let's ask Freddie to come
with us. We must check again the
Long Pond to see if there are any
more clues."

CHAPTER FIVE

Parker and Turnbull drove to Hampstead Heath.
The army let them through and they went to the
Long Pond again. Parker, Turnbull and Freddie looked
through the grass but they didn't find anything.

A soldier came up to them. "Why are you so
interested in that little bit of ground?" he said.
"A forensic team went over it all day yesterday and
they found nothing."

"We just came back for one more look," Parker said.

"Well, why don't you look under that rowing boat?
I don't think anybody bothered to look there,"
said the soldier.

"Thanks for your help," replied Agent Turnbull.

When Freddie turned the boat over he found a piece of metal with some numbers on it. "We've hit the jackpot!" said Freddie. "I can do wonders with this in the lab."

Back at the lab, Freddie did some tests on the metal. He looked puzzled.

"It's Plutonium A, a dangerous radioactive waste, but it looks as if it has melted into the frame of some kind of rocket. The rocket must have been about 20 metres long."

"Why would radioactive waste be in a rocket?" asked Turnbull. "Maybe it really was a terrorist attack!"

Parker frowned. "I need to go on the night train again," he said. "I need to check out that pool and the tall building there. It looked like a good place to launch a rocket from. We need to know what's going on there."

"It's too dangerous for you to go on your own," said Agent Turnbull. "We'll go together."

At three o'clock in the morning the two agents jumped
on to the night train. It took them to the secret plant.
Tonight, the searchlights were not on. Low red lights
lit up the radioactive rods in the water.

In the tall building beside the pool, the lights were all
on and the door was open. People were coming and
going, wearing special helmets and overalls.

"This is incredible!" said Turnbull. "I feel as if we're in
a James Bond film!"

As the two agents crept up to the building they heard people talking by the pool.

"Can Beta Two go up tonight?" somebody asked.

"The wind is too strong. We can't risk another failed mission over London," a voice replied.

Then the leader spoke. It was the voice of X.

"Beta Two will go up tomorrow night. Then we will send a rocket up every week. Within a year, the backlog will be clear," X said.

Parker and Turnbull could see him standing in the shadows near the pool. Turnbull felt a shiver go down her spine. "That's the man who came to my flat," she whispered.

"The man with no eyes?" asked Parker.

"The man who wants to kill us," she said.

X turned towards them. The agents' hearts missed a beat. Had he seen them? But the big shining glasses that covered his empty eye sockets were staring at nothing. They both felt silly for being frightened of a blind man.

"The Beta rockets will save this country from nuclear disaster. We can send all our nuclear waste deep into space. These rockets are our only hope for the future," X said. He began to smile.

"But what happens if we get another crash over London?" asked one of the scientists. "The rocket on Sunday was only carrying a little nuclear waste. Tomorrow's rocket will carry a hundred times that amount and if it fails it will destroy London."

"Don't worry," X said. "I trust your work."

"But it's not safe yet," said the scientist. "We need more time."

"If *I* say it is safe, then it *is* safe!" said X. He took off his glasses and began to polish them. Nobody said another word.

Parker and Turnbull had seen enough. They knew what they had to do. First they went to see Freddie. They told him what they had seen and what to do if anything happened to them.

Then they went to MI5 headquarters to see Commander Watson. They told him what they had seen and heard. Watson looked very worried. He told them that he would go straight to the Chief of MI5.

On the way out, Parker spoke to Commander Watson,
"If anything happens to myself or Agent Turnbull,
Sir, we have told somebody else. They will go to all the
newspapers and tell them what's going on. The rocket
programme must be stopped now. It's too dangerous."

Watson was very angry. "You are agents in the
Secret Service. You have no right to interfere with
government policy. You'll be disciplined for this,"
he said.

"We may be secret agents," said Agent Turnbull
angrily, "but it's our job to do what is right."

One hour later, five important people met in a room in Secret Service Headquarters.

"We have to stop the rocket project," said Belinda Williams, Chief of MI5.

"The government will be upset. They liked our work," said another commander.

"But it had to be top secret," said a man sitting in the shadows, polishing his glasses. "Agents Parker and Turnbull have destroyed all my work."

"They were only doing what they thought was their duty," said Commander Watson. They've been very brave. They've put their careers on the line."

The man in the shadows polished his glasses so hard that they broke.

"They've put more than their careers on the line!" he shouted. "I'll punish both of them in a way they'll never forget. Maybe not today or tomorrow, but one day soon."

Everyone went silent after his chilling words. Nobody dared to argue with X.

Two weeks later, Agent Parker went to the lab to show Freddie some new evidence. When he got there, all the blinds were pulled down and all the gas taps were running. Freddie was lying dead on the floor.

"Maybe this is just the beginning," whispered Agent Parker as he wiped the tears from his eyes. "From now on, none of us is safe."

GLOSSARY OF TERMS

dirty bomb chemical bomb

forensic scientific evidence which can be used to investigate a crime

Grade A Plutonium radioactive element

ID Identity cards

I can do wonders with this I can get a lot of valuable information from this

nuclear waste by products from a nuclear reactor

radioactive emitting radiation

plant a factory

state of emergency a dangerous situation in which the government puts the military in charge

to check out to investigate

to put their careers on the line to put their jobs at risk

to stick his nose in to interfere

we've hit the jackpot we're very lucky

QUIZ

1   What organisation do Agents Parker and Turnbull work for?

2   Where did the explosion take place?

3   What did Agent Parker find in the Long Pond?

4   Who did the agents go to see in the lab?

5   Why was the piece of metal dangerous?

6   What did the night train carry?

7   Who came to Turnbull's flat?

8   What does X do when he is angry?

9   Why was X sending rockets into space?

10   What did X threaten to do to Turnbull and Parker?

ABOUT THE AUTHOR

Paul Blum has taught for over 20 years in London inner-city schools.

I wrote The Extraordinary Files for my pupils so they've been tested by some fierce critics (you!). That's why I know you'll enjoy reading them.

I've made the stories edgy in terms of character and content and I've written them using the kind of fast-paced dialogue you'll recognise from television soaps. I hope you find The Extraordinary Files an interesting and easy-to-read collection of stories.

THE EXTRAORDINARY FILES

ROCKET INTO SPACE

By Paul Blum

A bomb explodes over London and the
Government blames it on terrorists.
Parker and Turnbull put their lives at risk to reveal
a project that should have stayed secret.

ISBN 978-1-84680-255-3

9 781846 802553

RISING ★ STARS

www.risingstars-uk.com